Monster Eyeballs

EGMONT

We bring stories to life

Book Band: Orange

First published in Great Britain 1999
This edition published 2002 by Egmont UK Limited
The Yellow Building, 1 Nicholas Road, London W11 4AN

ISBN 978 1 4052 0250 3
10 9 8 7 6
A CIP catalogue record for this title is available from the British Library
Printed and bound in Singapore
25690/23

EGMONT LUCKY COIN

Our story began over a century ago, when seventeen-year-old Egmont Harald Petersen found a coin in the street.

He was on his way to buy a flyswatter, a small hand-operated printing machine that he then set up in his tiny apartment.

The coin brought him such good luck that today Egmont has offices in over 30 countries around the world. And that lucky coin is still kept at the company's head offices in Denmark.

Jacqueline Wilson

Monster Eyeballs

Illustrated by Stephen Lewis

Blue Bananas

For

Thorne and Franca

J.W.

For

my mother

S.L.

Kate liked going to school.

Kate liked Art. She liked painting a picture of a lady in a long red dress.

She liked painting her nails red too.

Kate liked Story Time. One day the teacher read them *The Gingerbread Man*. Then she gave everyone a gingerbread man to eat.

Kate liked her best friend Amy most of all.

Help yourself!

There were a few bad things about school. Kate didn't like the toilets.

Kate didn't like being told off by

her teacher.

Most of all, Kate didn't like Mark. He was the biggest boy in the class. He was horrible.

I'm going to get you!
Help!

It was a good job Kate

had a best friend.

But one day Amy didn't come to school.

She had chickenpox and stayed at home.

Kate didn't feel happy without Amy.

Mark kept pestering her.

Mark couldn't do anything too terrible in the classroom – but at playtime Kate knew she was in for trouble. Big trouble!

Mark took Kate's chocolate at playtime.
Kate didn't have Amy to comfort her.
Kate missed Amy very much.

Amy wasn't back at school the next day – or the next – or the next. Kate didn't want to go to school without Amy.

Kate couldn't fool her mum. Mum knew Kate was missing Amy.

Mum gave Kate a special strawberry chocolate bar to eat at playtime.

Kate hid the chocolate in her pocket. But Kate couldn't fool Mark. 'I'm hungry,' he said. 'Give me some chocolate.'

Kate wanted to tell the teacher but she was too scared.

Kate told her big brother Robbie instead.

Robbie told Mark he'd twist *his* head off.

Mark told his big brother Andrew.

Robbie and Andrew had a big fight.

Robbie and Andrew had to stay in after school. But they didn't fight any more. They made friends.

Kate and Mark were amazed.

Mark was extra annoying in the classroom . . .

. . . Mark was extra annoying in the playground too.

Kate phoned her best friend

Amy to tell her.

'I'm all spotty and itchy,' said Amy. 'Mum's

painted the spots with pink stuff and she's

painted my nails pink to match.'

Kate was pleased when it was Saturday.

She didn't have to go to school.

Robbie was pleased too.

It was his birthday.

Robbie was having a party. He had invited three friends. Kate was invited too. She wore her special party frock and felt ever so grown up.

Robbie wore his new football strip. His friends wore football strips too. One of his friends was Andrew. Guess who Andrew brought with him!

NO! NO!
NO!

Robbie opened his presents. He got very excited.

Everyone got very excited.

Mum told them to go out in the garden and play football. Everyone liked that idea.

Kate wanted to play football too.
I want to be in goal.
Football!

Kate was good at football. She scored three goals.

Kate forgot she was wearing

her party frock.

Mum had made a very good birthday tea. Robbie had a special football birthday cake.

After tea Mum put on a cartoon.

Then she went to do the washing up and Robbie put on a different video. It was a very scary video about monsters.

Kate had seen it before.

She knew when to shut her eyes.

Mum got cross when she saw what they were watching. She switched the television off and told them to play party games. They played Squeak, Piggy, Squeak.

Kate was the Piggy.

They played murder in the dark.

Kate got murdered.

Then they played the Feely Game.
Everyone took turns to go into the kitchen, blindfolded. 'Feel the monster eyeballs, Kate,' said Robbie.

But Kate had played this game before. She knew they weren't really monster eyeballs.

Mark was the last to have a turn. He had never played the Feely Game before.

Mark hated the Feely Game!

Mark burst into tears. He had to have a cuddle with Kate's mum. Kate felt a bit sorry for him.

Mark didn't bother Kate at school after that birthday party. He wished he hadn't been so nasty to her before. He wanted to be her friend now!

Then Amy got better at last. Kate liked going to school again. 'Mark's O.K. now,' she said to Amy, 'but if he pesters us again I know just what to do.'